Cyril Bonhamy
and
Operation Ping

Jonathan Gathorne-Hardy

Cyril Bonhamy
and
Operation Ping

Illustrations by Quentin Blake

Jonathan Cape
Thirty-two Bedford Square London

First published 1985
Text © 1985 by Jonathan Gathorne-Hardy
Illustrations © 1985 by Quentin Blake

Jonathan Cape Ltd, 32 Bedford Square, London WC1B 3EL

British Library Cataloguing in Publication Data

Gathorne-Hardy, Jonathan
Cyril Bonhamy and Operation Ping.
I. Title
823'.914[J]   PZ7

ISBN 0-224-02287-3

Photoset in Great Britain by
Rowland Phototypesetting Ltd, Bury St Edmunds, Suffolk
and printed by St Edmundsbury Press
Bury St Edmunds, Suffolk

For Bec, Rupam and Joseph

Contents

"I Want Danger, Cyril."

"What do you think I'm supposed to do with *this*?" said Deirdre suddenly one winter's morning, thumping something down on to the breakfast table.

Cyril jumped nervously. "What is it, darling?" he said.

"It's the electricity bill," said Deirdre. "It's over £100. It's £105.92."

"Oh dear," said Cyril. There was rather a long silence in the big cold kitchen of their house in Wimbledon. Cyril stared longingly at the last sausage, but decided this wasn't the moment.

"Well," he said at last, beginning to sidle towards the door, "I think I'd better slip away and get on with my work."

"*No*," said Deirdre, looking up hurriedly from the bill still scrunched in her hand.

But she was too late. The door was shut and she could hear Cyril's footsteps in the distance rapidly ascending to the attic.

As she shot from the kitchen she heard the rattle

and creak as he pulled up the cheap metal ladder and slammed the trap door into his new attic library.

Deirdre stood underneath and banged the trap door with her broom. "Cyril," she called.

There was a short pause. "Yes, darling," shouted Cyril, his voice muffled.

"I want to talk to you about something, darling," called Deirdre.

There was another pause. Then she heard a shaking noise as Cyril reluctantly started to open the trap door and lower the ladder. The shaking and rattling grew louder and then louder. Nothing happened to the trap door. Now there came a tremendous rattling and clattering and crashing and bumping. Cyril seemed to be jumping up and down on the door. Then he stopped.

"I'm afraid it's stuck again, darling," he called down in a relieved voice. "You'll have to call the Fire Brigade."

Wearily, Deirdre put the broom back against the wall and went downstairs to ring 999.

In a way it was her fault the ladder went wrong. When Cyril had received his money from the French Government, he had immediately turned the attic into a huge library. For weeks workers had tramped up and down the stairs. Books had arrived by post and by taxi; sometimes by lorry.

Cyril wrote books, and wrote about books and talked about books on telly. Deirdre could see he had to have *some* books, but why so many books? The house was full of books already. Sometimes Deirdre thought she hated books.

And then one day she found out what it was all costing. "Cyril!" she cried, bursting into tears. "This means we're going to be poor again."

Cyril hurriedly cancelled two lorry loads of books arriving that afternoon. He also cancelled his order for some special shelves that hung from the ceiling. And instead of the fine staircase he'd planned with banisters and knobs, he'd put in the cheap tin flapjack affair which rattled and clattered and stuck.

When the Fire Brigade arrived the Chief Fireman was quite cross.

"This is the tenth time you've called us out this month," he said to Deirdre. "There are people burning to death while we get Mr Bonhamy out of his library."

When they'd unstuck the ladder, he said, "I'm afraid I'll have to charge you £3.50 this time, Mrs Bonhamy."

Usually the fuss of the ladder and the Fire Brigade made Deirdre forget about the bills she wanted to show Cyril, but the £3.50 reminded her.

"Cyril," she said, pushing him firmly into a chair beside her at the breakfast table and opening the biscuit tin of bills, "Cyril, we've got to talk about money."

Cyril listened unhappily while, as so often before, Deirdre explained about the bills. His mind began to wander. He thought longingly of his big new library with its books and the new, two-bar electric fire. It was quite a shock when he heard Deirdre say, ". . . and so what shall we *do*?"

"Do?" said Cyril. "How do you mean, *do*? Do what about what? Oh yes, *do*," he went on hurriedly, recognising the expression which was beginning to form on Deirdre's face. "Of course – *do*. Do-de-do-de-do. Well, of course, I've been thinking about it a lot. There are several things we could do."

Cyril stopped. His mind was quite blank. After a long pause he said, "But I think I know the best solution. Don't worry, darling. I shall write another book."

"A BOOK!" shrieked Deirdre at the top of her voice. She suddenly wanted to hit Cyril as hard as she could with the biscuit tin of bills. But then, as she always did when he said he'd write another book, she managed to calm down. She loved Cyril. And she was proud of his books. It was just a pity they never made any money.

"The thing is we need money *now*," she said as gently as she could. "Couldn't you try and get a nice job, Cyril? After all, Christmas is coming up and you are a fully trained Father Christmas now. Why don't you get a nice cosy job as a Father Christmas at a store?"

"Oh honestly, Deirdre," said Cyril crossly, "what a ridiculous suggestion. You know very well what happened last time. I'm not going to get a Father Christmas job again if it kills me – which it probably would."

But sitting up in the attic library, he thought perhaps he really ought to try and do something. Not become a Father Christmas. Being a store Father Christmas meant, as far as he could see, more or less certain death. But perhaps a new book wasn't a bad idea. After all, some writers were millionaires. He'd give his publisher a ring.

Mr Hoff was a tall, very thin man with a shiny bald head and large popping-out eyes like marbles. He had long, thin, bony fingers with large, knobbly knuckles.

"Morning, Bonhamy," he said the next day, "good to see you. What can I do for you? How's things?"

"Well, actually, things aren't too good," said Cyril rather gloomily. He began to explain in a rambling way about the biscuit tin of bills and how worried Deirdre got.

"What I really need is some money," he ended. Adding hurriedly, because he knew Mr Hoff hated talk about money, "Not much of course. I thought a little, a few hundred, for a new book. Unless of course the last one is doing so well I needn't bother," said Cyril, brightening.

"Well I'm afraid the last one *isn't* doing too well," said Mr Hoff, beginning to look gloomy in his turn. He picked up a small piece of paper from his desk. "In fact, so far, I'm afraid we've only sold fifty-three copies."

"Fifty-three eh?" said Cyril, thinking that didn't sound too bad. "I wonder who bought them. Would it be possible to meet them?"

"I doubt it," said Mr Hoff, still staring glumly at the piece of paper. "But never mind. Everyone thought it was very good. Now – a new book. What had you in mind?"

"Well," said Cyril, who had nothing in mind, "what do you think? How about a book about the medieval Beebles of Nice?"

"Beebles?" said Mr Hoff, puzzled. "What are Beebles?"

"It's French for Bibles," said Cyril, but he could see Mr Hoff wasn't too keen. "Well, recently I've got very interested in the history of flower pots."

"Flower pots?" said Mr Hoff, beginning to look round. "I don't think many people are interested in flower pots." He started to pull his long fingers so that the knuckles made loud cracking noises.

"Well, we needn't stick to flower pots," said Cyril. "I could include ink pots and chimney pots and jam pots and honey pots. In fact," said Cyril rather wildly, seeing that Mr Hoff was looking less and less interested, "how about throwing in chamber pots and tea pots and coffee pots and lobster pots, pepper pots, salt pots, rice pots, ice pots, Henrietta Maria pots . . ."

"Henrietta Maria pots?" interrupted Mr Hoff, cracking another few knuckles. "What are they? But no, Cyril, I don't think we'd get many readers for a book on pots, even Henrietta Maria pots, whatever they may be. I doubt we'd even get fifty-three readers for a book on pots. No, Cyril, what I think you should do is something *completely different*."

Mr Hoff now stared at Cyril for some minutes with his bulging eyes. Then he stood up and began to walk up and down.

"What I'd like — what I'd pay good money for — is something like a spy story," he said. "Or something about drugs. How about the things you see on telly, Cyril – well, I don't, but my son and daughter do and sometimes I see them by chance. You know what I mean, Cyril. Films about murder and crime in America, lots of deaths and danger and violence and bullets and car chases.

"Wheeeeeee*screeeeeeech*!" suddenly cried Mr Hoff, whirling on his toes and making a noise like brakes.

Then all at once he crouched low and began to advance across the room towards Cyril with his huge bony hands outstretched as if he were going to strangle him. "Did you see *The Texas Chain Saw Massacre?*" he asked, his eyes gleaming. "I did – quite by chance of course, my son got the video. Masses of blood, Cyril, masses and masses of blood and car chases. How about being spun to death in a launderette dryer?" said Mr Hoff in an excited voice, coming nearer and nearer as Cyril shrank nervously back into his chair. "Or cooked alive in a microwave oven, or thumped to bits by a pneumatic drill or – just – squashed – flat – like – THAT!" shouted Mr Hoff, now very excited indeed, clapping his hands together in front of Cyril's nose.

"Ah well," said Mr Hoff, panting a bit as he went back to his desk, "you know what I mean, Cyril – plenty of blood and car chases and danger. What do you think?"

"I think it's a marvellous idea," said Cyril, still trembling. "The only thing is I don't really like danger. In fact, I absolutely hate it. But I do like microwave ovens," he quickly added in case Mr Hoff should decide not to give him any money.

So it was agreed. Cyril was to write a book about danger and bullets and blood and car chases. He was to write out the plot, just a few pages saying what would happen in the book, and bring it to Mr Hoff next week.

"And when you've done that," said Mr Hoff airily, "I don't think we'll find that money is really a problem. No problem at all."

Walking back to the Underground, still feeling faintly sick at the idea of all the blood and bullets and danger, Cyril tried to think if there wasn't some other way of making money. Perhaps after all he might have a go at being a store Father Christmas again.

But at that very moment, in Scotland Yard, a top-level, highly-secret meeting was taking place at which important men were discussing things far worse than the chain saw massacres and car chases of Mr Hoff – a meeting which, quite soon, was to have the most terrible effect on Cyril's life.

Task Force Ping

"Now gentlemen," said Commander Henderson, Chief of the Metropolitan Police, "let me introduce you. This, of course, is Mr Underline, the Minister of Defence; on my left is Colonel Clout of the Special Air Services, the SAS."

Quickly Commander Henderson went round the table introducing the few other very important officials, and then sat down to let the Minister of Defence explain what the meeting was about.

Mr Underline was tall and thin with a flat face and piercing blue eyes. He stood up and looked round the table.

"I hope I needn't remind you that what I am about to say is Top Secret," he said. "No one must repeat a word of it to anyone." The six men listening to him nodded gravely. They were all used to keeping Top Secrets. There were so many things Commander Henderson wasn't allowed to tell anyone he sometimes wondered how he managed to talk at all.

"You will have read in the papers how the terrible

drug war in Malaysia and Thailand has nearly ended," the Minister said, leaning forward across the table.

He described how months of desperate fighting in the jungles had gradually driven the drug smugglers' leader, the evil Abbot Ping Po, nearer and nearer the coast. Finally he had fled with the last 300 of his warrior monks to a little rocky island in the shark-infested seas off Malaysia.

"He has built himself a fortress equipped with every modern weapon," said the Minister. "I'm told he has Exocet missiles, radar, plastic saucer, teacup and soup plate mines, laser beam rockets and even chemical fog. The Malaysians can do nothing." He paused and looked at the serious faces round the table.

Only one man looked puzzled. Young Colonel Clout of the SAS, with his short red hair and little moustache, had his hand up.

"Excuse me, Minister," he said. "I know some of those weapons are pretty good: a teacup mine can be absolutely appalling, and as for chemical fog, well the least said the better. But surely the whole Malaysian army against 300 monks, however tough, could do *something*? I mean, how about a few well-directed bombs?"

"Good thinking, Clout," said the Minister, "good thinking. But you've reckoned without the devilish cunning of Abbot Ping Po. He has chosen the Island of Pung. On the Island of Pung is the 2,000-year-old Monastery of Pung. This is a very holy place. It is one of the holiest places in the whole Far East – far too holy to attack. Abbot Ping Po is as safe as houses."

"What makes the place so important?" asked Colonel Clout.

"No one knows," said the Minister. "That is, no one in the West. Not exactly that is – it's some ancient relic too holy to be mentioned by name. It's been a secret for 2,000 years, passed down to a few monks each century. But it must be pretty extraordinary. The Malaysians have told me none of the countries out there would dare to attack Pung. They'd have all the other countries on them like a ton of coconuts.

"And that is why they've asked us to help. The Prime Minister is taking a personal interest and has asked me to arrange it. I thought it seemed a job for your lads in the SAS, Clout. What do you say?"

Here Colonel Clout, who'd been listening with great interest, began to look doubtful. "When would you want us to go, Minister?" he asked.

"Oh, right away," said the Minister. "This is an emergency. Top priority."

Colonel Clout scratched his head. "Well usually I'd say yes like a shot," he said. "My boys are simply itching for a scrap. But, as you know, we lost four officers on that African job. And both Major de Biff and Captain Toggle are in hospital with fractured skulls. Jim de Biff is second-in-command and would lead an assault. He's also the training officer. If it was just a hi-jacking or an Embassy job, or some terrorist shenanigans, I wouldn't think twice. But this is something big. It's probably the biggest thing the SAS has ever tackled. I wouldn't like to trust one of the younger officers."

He stopped. The seven men exchanged worried glances.

"What about you, Henderson?" said the Minister, turning to the Chief of Police. "Can you supply Clout with someone? Some daring young police officer with plenty of guts and go? Some brave leader or other, a man of dash and spirit, sick of being a humdrum police officer, sick of London – ho! ho!" laughed the Minister, tossing back a long lock of fair hair, "I've half a mind to go myself."

Commander Henderson thought hard. Apart from himself, he could think of no one. And then suddenly, in a flash, the solution came to him.

"Gentlemen," he cried, "I know our man! If we can get him – Cyril Bonhamy!"

There was a short puzzled silence. The Minister looked at Commander Henderson. So did Colonel Clout. Quickly, Commander Henderson explained.

"Mr Bonhamy is one of the bravest men I've ever met," he said. "And also one of the strongest. He's a small man. Very small. Don't be deceived. As strong as a horse. At the same time, he's one of the most modest men I've ever met. I could see his name meant little to you."

"It rang a bell," said Colonel Clout vaguely.

Commander Henderson described how Cyril had once captured three dangerous Arab terrorists single-handed, as well as blowing up their desert fort. Since then, just for fun, for the sheer love of danger, he'd destroyed the gangs of two of the world's most wanted criminals – the notorious Madam Big and the terrible Pierre Melon. He was like an entire SAS force on his own.

"Madam Big?" said Colonel Clout. "I'm sure I've heard some of the older men talk about her. Didn't this chap Bonhamy do some terrific jumps or other?"

"That's it," said Commander Henderson. "Jumping and leaping are Bonhamy's speciality. He can jump like a deer, leap like a ballet dancer. You could say Bonhamy is a mixture between a ballet dancer and a bomb."

Everyone was delighted. "Clearly this is our man," said the Minister. "A mixture between a ballet dancer and a bomb – just what we were looking for."

He stood up. "Right Clout," he said, "I suggest we call it 'Task Force Ping'. Be ready to move in five days. Henderson, you get this fellow Bonhamy. Money's no object – we'll give him full service pay, more if he wants it. Any questions?"

"There is just one thing," said Colonel Clout. "Does this chap Bonhamy keep himself fit? Five days isn't long to get ready. It's going to be tough, dangerous work."

"Oh, I think we can be sure Bonhamy keeps himself in pretty good shape," said Commander Henderson confidently.

Cyril was at that moment asleep in front of the living room fire. Deirdre, on hearing that money was more or less on its way, had cooked a delicious lunch as a reward – roast chicken, sausages, Brussels sprouts and masses of bread sauce.

With difficulty, and rather irritated, Cyril struggled out of his chair to speak to Commander Henderson. He was quite surprised to be rung up by him but not all that surprised. Commander Henderson admired Cyril's books and had twice had him out to tea so that he could sign copies of them.

He was, however, surprised that Commander Henderson wanted to see him at once.

"What, *now*?" said Cyril, looking at the Coalite glowing hot and cheerful in the fireplace. "As a matter of fact, I'm rather busy at the moment."

"Well, tomorrow morning then," said Commander Henderson hastily. He didn't want to upset Cyril. "I'll send a car."

"That's very kind. What's it about? My books?"

"No, something quite different," said Commander Henderson. "But it's Top Secret. I can't tell you on the phone."

And so, next morning at ten-thirty Cyril found himself at Scotland Yard.

"Sit down," said Commander Henderson. "Have some tea, have some coffee. A cake?" He'd decided to take it slowly. "Tell me, Bonhamy," he said cunningly, "what are you writing at the moment?"

"Well, actually, I wanted to write a book about the old Beebles of Nice," began Cyril.

"Beebles?" said Commander Henderson. "What are Beebles?"

"It's French for Bibles," said Cyril wearily. Sometimes he thought he was the only person in the world who spoke French properly.

23

"But in the end," he went on, with a sudden feeling of panic, "I agreed to write a sort of thriller. You know – blood, car chases, pneumatic drills, chain saws." He went on about car chases and drugs and danger until all at once Commander Henderson interrupted him.

He looked steadily at Cyril and said very distinctly and slowly, "If it's danger you want, Bonhamy, I think I can give you plenty of *that*. Oh yes, I can certainly give you danger."

"Really?" said Cyril, immediately becoming interested. It occurred to him that Commander Henderson might be the solution to his problem. Obviously, Commander Henderson led a life chock-full of danger. A ghastly life, in fact.

But perhaps the answer would simply be to get Commander Henderson to tell him about it. Or else follow him about for a few months – at a safe distance of course – and then write down what happened.

"Well, I suppose danger *is* what I want," he said. "Provided of course there isn't any danger, if you see what I mean. And I imagine your life is full of it – car chases and the like, chain saws, microwave ovens. Tell me about it."

At once Commander Henderson embarked on the complicated story of Task Force Ping. Quite quickly Cyril saw it was nothing to do with the police. But gradually he realised that Commander Henderson was suggesting that he, Cyril, should play some part in the venture.

And suddenly he realised how brilliant this was.

Commander Henderson meant him to go as an observer, a sort of war correspondent. He would go and watch what went on and then write a book about it.

"Excuse me," said Cyril, interrupting Commander Henderson, "but do I understand you right – do you mean I'm to be part of this Ping thing?"

"That's it," said Commander Henderson.

"And could I write about it?" said Cyril.

"Oh I expect so," said Commander Henderson. "Yes, I'm sure you could."

"I see," said Cyril. "Could you just explain it all again? I'm afraid I wasn't really listening. This Abbot Ping Pong is on some island – why?"

"Po," said Commander Henderson. "Abbot Ping Po." And once again he explained how the terrible drug smuggler Abbot Ping Po, with his 300 warrior monks, had taken refuge on the sacred Island of Pung. How no one from Malaysia could attack him because it contained something so holy that practically no one knew what it was. And how Cyril and the SAS were to go in and, as Commander Henderson put it, "take him out".

Cyril wanted to be quite sure there was no misunderstanding. "And I can write about it – I mean a book?" he said again.

"Yes," said Commander Henderson.

"All right," said Cyril. "Obviously I'll play no part in any rough stuff. But I'd feel quite safe with the SAS." He'd been very relieved to hear about the SAS. He remembered them from Madam Big days – a gang of thumping thugs hurling stun bombs.

"But as long as I can write about this fellow Pung-Pong or Ping or whatever he's called – yes, I agree."

Commander Henderson laughed at Cyril's little joke about not taking part in the rough stuff.

"I wouldn't be in Abbot Ping Po's shoes for all the tea in China," he said. And then, after a pause and feeling rather awkward, he said, "By the way, Bonhamy, excuse me asking, but, ahem, how's your shape? Pretty good, eh?"

"My *shape*?" said Cyril blankly. He didn't really like people talking about his shape, which was more or less round. Deirdre quite often said he was too fat and made him go for a walk on Wimbledon Common or took a sausage off his plate. But he didn't suppose Commander Henderson could be rude enough to mean that. "How do you mean, my shape?"

"Well, you know, *shape*," said Commander Henderson, getting more and more embarrassed. He quickly did two press-ups to show what he meant. "Pretty good I imagine – I mean perfect."

"I don't know about *perfect*," said Cyril, feeling rather irritated, although he still hadn't the faintest idea what Commander Henderson was getting at. "It's good enough."

"Exactly," said Commander Henderson quickly. "Just as I thought. Sorry I brought it up." And then, to make Cyril completely happy again, he said, "You'll be needing some money, I suppose?"

"Will I?" said Cyril. "Oh, you mean for clothes – sandals and things. Yes, I will."

"How much?" said Commander Henderson.

"Well . . ." said Cyril slowly. He'd suddenly found he was thinking about the hanging bookshelves in his library which he'd had to cancel, and the nice, non-stick staircase he'd wanted to build. He took a deep breath. "Eight hundred pounds," he said.

"As *well* as your salary?" said Commander Henderson, a bit surprised.

"Salary?" said Cyril. It hadn't occurred to him he might be paid to write this book, except of course by Mr Hoff.

"Quite, quite," said Commander Henderson rapidly, terrified that Cyril might suddenly say no to the whole idea. "I'll see to it at once. Eight hundred pounds and a month's salary in advance."

When Cyril had gone, Commander Henderson rang up Colonel Clout.

"Well, that's fine, Colonel," he said, "Bonhamy accepted like a shot. As you said – itching for a scrap. Can't wait to get his hands on them. And as for fitness, no need to worry about *that* at any rate. Fit as a fiddle. Pink of condition. Hard as nails. Tough as old boots. In fact," said Commander Henderson, getting rather carried away, "Bonhamy quite frightened me to tell you the truth. Handshake of a gorilla – regular bone crusher."

Colonel Clout was quite surprised when the bone crusher himself arrived at the SAS barracks the next day. Commander Henderson had said he was small, but this Bonhamy chap was, well, *very* small.

To Cyril, the SAS officers to whom he was introduced all seemed huge. He didn't mind. The huger the better as far as he was concerned. There was only one man he didn't particularly like.

"I'd like you to meet Sergeant–Major Rude," said Colonel Clout. "RSM Rude will be your second–in–command. He was hoping you'd be able to teach him some of your tricks."

Cyril looked at the giant figure in front of him. He had a round, red face, with little piggy eyes and black hair cut short as a toothbrush. He had thick fingers like sausages. It didn't seem to him that RSM Rude would ever learn to write a book. He didn't really think that RSM Rude would even learn to hold a pen.

"I doubt it," he said.

RSM Rude drew himself up. He had a violent temper, and he in his turn had taken an instant dislike to Cyril. "I beg pardon, sir," he said. "I 'ope you can rely on me, sir."

"Oh yes, yes yes yes yes of course," said Cyril hastily, who'd noticed the enormous sausage fingers bunching up into something resembling fists. "Oh yes, Mr Rude. It's just I happen to like doing that sort of thing on my own."

A murmur of appreciation ran round the group of officers. This was the sort of spirit they liked – a man who'd dare take out the frightful Abbot Ping Po on his very own.

"Well, he's got guts, that's certain," said Captain Crump when Colonel Clout had taken Cyril to be measured for his uniform.

"You don't think he's, er, a bit on the small side,

sir?" said one of the lieutenants, a strapping lad of six feet nine inches.

But two of the officers could just remember the great fight with Madam Big. They described the incredible death-defying leap with which Cyril had lured her to her doom.

"Yes," said Captain Crump, "the colonel told me of the leaps this man Bonhamy can do."

"A sort of kung fu I suppose," said the lieutenant thoughtfully.

"You'd better pass the word round to the men," Captain Crump said to RSM Rude. "You know – kung fu expert, gave the chop to Madam Big. They could be a bit surprised when they first see this Bonhamy chappy in the flesh so to speak. We don't want them to get him wrong."

"Right you are, sir," said RSM Rude, saluting. He thought Cyril was a right twit, a proper shrimp. As far as he was concerned, Mr Cyril – kung fu – Madam Big – Bonhamy could take a running jump off the nearest cliff.

Since all the men in Task Force Ping were at least six feet high and most of them were taller, they found that nothing fitted Cyril. Everything would have to be made. And made very quickly. Task Force Ping was to leave in four days' time.

"I don't see why I need any uniform for what I'm going to do," said Cyril, as yet another hat was discarded as too big.

"Oh, ha ha ha ha ha," laughed Colonel Clout, "good one, Bonhamy, good one. But, apart from all the reasons you know better than I do, did Commander Henderson explain that you were to be a major in the SAS?"

"No," said Cyril.

"Yes," said Colonel Clout. "For as long as Task Force Ping goes on it'll be Major Bonhamy."

"Really?" said Cyril. "Major Bonhamy eh?" He felt rather pleased. Deirdre would be proud of him.

Deirdre was not just proud of him; she realised the SAS could solve all their problems.

"But couldn't you join the SAS properly, Cyril?" she said. "It's such a good salary, and this Colonel Clout sounds charming."

"I don't know about that," said Cyril. "I don't suppose they'd want more than one book written about them. After they've dealt with this Pong or Pung, or whatever his name is, that'll be that."

Deirdre planned to have a word with Colonel Clout later. But there were more urgent things to do at once.

"We must get you some nice clothes to wear off duty," she said. "Malaysia is the tropics, Cyril. Nothing you've got is suitable."

Deirdre bought him two smart white suits, three pairs of white shorts, two pairs of sandals, a black silk dressing gown for evening wear, some swimming trunks, a Li-lo for sunbathing on, and a dozen short-sleeved shirts in gay Tahitian colours.

"Don't you think they're a bit bright?" said Cyril, looking dubiously at the brilliant orange, blue, green and purple whirls.

"Oh no," said Deirdre, "it's what people wear in

the tropics. We'll have two of those nice floppy sun hats," she said to the assistant.

She bought a set of beach towels, sun glasses and some gym shoes.

"Steady on," said Cyril. Soon there wouldn't be any money left for his shelves and new non-stick attic stairs. "Why are you getting gym shoes?"

"For when you play tennis," said Deirdre.

"I can't play tennis," said Cyril crossly. He pushed the gym shoes towards the assistant. Deirdre reached over and pulled them firmly back.

They had to buy three large leatherette suitcases to hold everything. On the way out Deirdre suddenly saw a display of sun parasols on special offer.

"*No*," said Cyril. "Deirdre, this is the SAS. They are soldiers. I'm going to be Major Bonhamy. I can't turn up with a parasol."

"You most certainly can," said Deirdre. "It's the tropics, Cyril. You know how easily you get sunburnt, and what happens then? I've no doubt the SAS have things to protect themselves from the sun."

Cyril thought of RSM Rude. He thought RSM Rude was very unlikely to have a parasol. He watched wearily as Deirdre carried the two yellow and green parasols over to the "Pay Here" counter. One of them had tassels.

Sunburn reminded Dierdre of several other things. On the way back to Wimbledon she stopped at a chemist and bought Dettol ointment, Elastoplast, sun-tan cream, aspirins and stuff for wasp stings.

The next day Cyril went back to the SAS barracks

to try on his uniform. Everything was ready. His peaked hat was a little too large but the rest fitted perfectly; dress uniform, ordinary uniform, tropical uniform. They'd even made a special frogman's wet suit for him, covered in loops for stun bombs, hooks for sub-machine guns and rifles, pouches for grenades. The flippers fitted like gloves.

"I don't suppose I'll use this much," said Cyril. He didn't like to admit he could really only float on his back and even then he usually had water wings.

Colonel Clout explained that he and the other officers were to fly out immediately. They'd have a close look at the Island of Pung and plan the attack.

"We'll try some night landings and test the defences," he said.

The men, with Major Bonhamy in command, were to come out more slowly by boat. This would give them time to get used to the heat and also do some more training.

"I'd like you to run that, Bonhamy," said Colonel Clout. "Assault course stuff, advance under smoke, under fire, parachute drops – can you handle that?"

Cyril looked at him blankly. He hadn't the faintest idea what he was talking about. "Handle it?" he said.

"RSM Rude knows the drill," said Colonel Clout.

"Oh, RSM Rude is coming on the boat is he?" said Cyril. He'd rather hoped RSM Rude would be flying out with the officers.

"Yes," said Colonel Clout. "Splendid fellow. But I'd like you to teach them some of your tricks, Bonhamy – those leaps you do and so on."

Cyril didn't answer. The SAS clearly didn't have the faintest idea what was involved in writing a book. It wouldn't have surprised him to learn that some of them couldn't read or write at all. RSM Rude probably signed his name with the end of one of his large, sausage thumbs.

They were to sail in two days. Cyril had one thing left to do. He rang his old friend Professor Nic Hill at the British Museum and asked if they had any books on the sacred Island of Pung.

"How odd," said Professor Hill. "If you'd rung me a month ago, I'd have had to say – very little. But they recently discovered some very ancient Greek parchments in a grave near Athens. They are copies of very old Chinese writings and are all about the Island of Pung. They haven't even been translated. If I send you some Xerox copies, could you do it for us?"

"My Greek is a bit rusty," said Cyril, "but I'll try."

The copies of the precious parchments arrived that evening. Cyril took them up at once to his attic library.

The Greek was difficult but he could just read it. There was even a plan of the ancient Monastery of Pung. Cyril peered at it excitedly through his glasses. This was going to be very interesting indeed.

Unfortunately, at that moment, Deirdre shouted up the stairs that supper was ready.

She had spent the afternoon doing some last-minute shopping for him, including a pair of water wings. She had also cooked a special goodbye meal of roast beef, with Yorkshire pudding and roast potatoes.

"I do hope you'll be all right, darling," she said, heaping a second helping on to his plate. "You don't think there's any danger do you?"

"Oh gracious me, no," said Cyril airily. "At least, not for me. I shall be quite safe, protected by those great thugs in the SAS. And I certainly shan't go anywhere until any fighting is well over. I'll spend most of the time in my cabin. Could you pass the gravy?"

"Well, mind you're careful," said Deirdre. "I bought some of that black stuff in case you get a touch of the collywobbles."

Deirdre had in fact bought so many extra things that they had to buy a fourth leatherette suitcase next morning, even though the SAS had given him a kitbag.

When he had packed, Cyril put on his new uniform. Deirdre agreed the hat was a bit large, but she said it suited him. In fact, she thought he looked so smart she went and got the camera and took several photographs.

Cyril was just getting into the taxi when he let out a cry, "Good heavens – all those parchments about the Island of Pung are still in the library."

"Don't shut the trap door, darling," Deirdre yelled up the stairs after him. If the trap door jammed again, as it usually did, he'd miss the train to Southampton, where he was joining the ship. Besides, she didn't want to see the Chief Fireman again quite so soon.

While he was in his library Cyril took out a book about the flowers of Malaysia and a Chinese dictionary and put them with the copies of the parchments into his briefcase.

There was so much luggage that one case and the kitbag had to go in front with the driver. The other three cases and the briefcase went in the back with Cyril.

He kissed Deirdre goodbye and told the driver to go to Waterloo station. Then he sat back and opened the book on Malaysian flowers.

Cyril had begun the most frightening and dangerous adventure of his whole life.

RSM Rude

Trouble began almost as soon as he boarded the cruiser HMS *Nelson* at five o'clock.

RSM Rude was waiting for him at the top of the gangway. As Cyril came up the RSM sprang to attention.

"Good arternoon, *sir*," he said loudly, saluting.

Cyril saluted back, knocking his hat over his eyes.

"Could you send someone to get my luggage from the taxi down there," he said.

RSM Rude turned to a tall SAS soldier standing to attention by his side. "This is Private Coggins, sir," he said. "Your batman. Private Coggins will take care of your uniform and suchlike. Coggins, go and get Major Bonhamy's kitbag from the taxi."

Coggins had to make three journeys. RSM Rude stared in amazement at the row of suitcases and the briefcase.

"I'm sorry, sir," he said, "but regulations clearly state for officers and men – one kitbag only."

"I can't help that," said Cyril briskly. He wasn't

37

having any nonsense from RSM Rude. "Will you take me to my cabin? Coggins, bring the luggage."

In the cabin RSM Rude once again tried to protest. "I'm sorry, Major Bonhamy," he said, "but it is the custom in the SAS that officers and men observe the same rules and regulations. Most of this luggage must go back."

"None of this luggage is going back," said Cyril crossly. "For goodness' sake, RSM Rude, obviously none of your regulations applies to me. Now please go. I want to unpack."

"Private Coggins will unpack for you, sir," said RSM Rude.

"No he won't," said Cyril. He had no desire for Private Coggins or anyone else to see some of the things Deirdre had bought him. Certainly not the parasols or the water wings. And it was probably better to hide the short-sleeved shirts with their gay Tahitian colours for a while. "That will be all," he said.

RSM Rude stared down at him. He wanted to pick Cyril up and throw him out of the cabin window. After a moment, he managed to take a deep breath. He saluted. "Yes, sir," he said.

Cyril's cabin was large and comfortable, with an attached bathroom, lots of cupboards and a big desk. The window, which would soon look out over the ocean, now looked upon Southampton docks.

When he'd unpacked, Cyril took a little stroll. Everywhere he went sailors and soldiers saluted him. Cyril got more and more bored saluting back and after a while just vaguely waved at them. Even so, his arm was quite tired when he got back to his cabin.

He had two visitors during the evening before supper. The first was announced by a gentle tap on the door and the tall, bearded figure of Captain Silkin stepped in.

"Welcome aboard, Major Bonhamy," said the captain. "I trust you'll eat with the officers of HMS *Nelson* during the voyage."

Cyril said he'd be delighted to. Captain Silkin said he could see Cyril was busy and supper was at eight o'clock. He bowed and went out.

The second visit was from RSM Rude. There was a sharp bang on the door, it flew open and the huge, heavy figure took two clumping steps in and crashed his boots together. "Sir!" yelled RSM Rude, saluting.

Cyril put his hands to his ears, wincing. "Please, RSM Rude," he said, "I'm not deaf. What do you want?"

"Men of SAS Task Force Ping ready for inspection, *sir*," he said, saluting again.

"What do you mean?" said Cyril.

"Don't you want to inspect the men, sir?" said RSM Rude.

"Inspect them?" said Cyril, rather surprised. "Why? What on earth should I inspect?"

"Their bed spaces," said RSM Rude, surprised in his turn. "Their bunks, their kits, their weapons."

"I can't think why," said Cyril. "No, I don't."

There was a silence. RSM Rude stared at Cyril out of his piggy eyes. At last he said, "Well, will you inspect them at Muster Parade in the morning?"

"I suppose so, if you insist," said Cyril, hardly listening. "Now look, RSM Rude, I'm very busy. And please don't make that horrible noise with your boots when you go out this time."

RSM Rude stared at him in silence again. He couldn't even bring himself to say, "Yes, sir." He just saluted and left.

Cyril found at supper that Captain Silkin was a most delightful man. He was interested in books and in fact had read several of those that Cyril had written. He was astonished to find it was Cyril Bonhamy the writer in charge of the 200 crack SAS troops of Task Force Ping.

"I'd no idea you were a soldier, Bonhamy," he said.

"I'm not," said Cyril, helping himself to another chop; "I'm just here to write a book about them. I shan't do any fighting or anything like that."

Captain Silkin was also an expert on Malaysian flowers and trees.

"You'll see the Weeping Rope Weed," he said. "Grows 300 feet or more. And the Giant Pin Bush – spikes five inches long and hard as steel. I must say, Bonhamy, I wish I could come and explore the Island of Pung with you."

"I don't see why you shouldn't, Captain Silkin," said Cyril. "Once RSM Rude and his men have made it safe, we can explore it together."

Cyril went to bed early. Just before he fell asleep he heard the muffled blast of a siren and then a steady shudder as HMS *Nelson* set out for the open seas.

It was still dark when he was roughly shaken awake.

"Who's that?" said Cyril sleepily.

"It's me, sir, Private Coggins," said a voice. "It's time to get up."

"*Time to get up?*" said Cyril crossly, sitting up. "It's the middle of the night." He lay down again.

"RSM Rude said to wake you at seven o'clock, sir," said Private Coggins. "Muster Parade is in half an hour."

Cyril groaned. He felt he'd only been asleep about ten minutes. But Private Coggins had turned on the light and was setting out his uniform. He'd even put the rifle Cyril had been given across the chair.

"I'm not carrying that thing around," said Cyril. He got out of bed and went to throw the rifle into one of the cupboards.

In the bathroom shaving he thought – I wish that man Rude would leave me alone. I'm not getting up at this hour every morning.

The men of Task Force Ping were drawn up in three long ranks on deck. It was grey and cold in the early morning. As far as the eye could see there was nothing but grey, cold sea. Cyril stood shivering as RSM Rude came marching towards him across the deck.

Crash! went RSM Rude's boots as he stopped with a bang in front of Cyril. Smack! went his hands as he hit his forehead with a salute.

"Task Force Ping present and ready for inspection, *sir*," he bellowed.

"All right, all right, no need to make such a

noise," said Cyril waving back at him. "You lead the way."

Following RSM Rude between the ranks he wondered again what he was supposed to inspect *for*? Fleas? Lice? Dirty fingernails? In fact, almost all he could inspect were their belts, since that was about where his eyes came.

The giant men of the SAS were too well trained to laugh or stare. Nevertheless, out of the corners of their eyes they looked in amazement at the little figure trotting in front of them, stopping every now and again to peer at their belts. Was this really the man who'd captured Madam Big? The man who, according to RSM Rude, was to teach them his deadly leaps, more terrible than anything in kung fu?

When they'd finished, Cyril gave his wave salute to RSM Rude and said, "Nothing wrong that I can see − at least, not with their belts. You get on with whatever you've got to do. I'm going to have breakfast and then I'll go back to bed." And with another wave salute he hurried back below decks to the warmth and safety of his cabin.

However, he had hardly returned to it after a delicious breakfast when there came a bang on the door and, with a familiar and painful crashing of boots, RSM Rude thumped in.

"Training programme, sir," he said, thrusting a sheet of paper at Cyril.

Cyril looked at it: assault course, battle training, parachute jumping, night attack. It meant nothing to him, except it all looked very dangerous.

"Very good," he said. "Now, if you don't mind, I didn't get much sleep last night."

"Sleep?" said RSM Rude. "Aren't you going to take charge of the men?"

"No," said Cyril.

RSM Rude took a step forward until he loomed hugely over Cyril at his desk.

"In the SAS, Major Bonhamy, we have a tradition," he said. "The officers not only lead the men into battle, they lead them in training. This morning, after the assault course, it is unarmed combat. This arternoon parachute jumping. I *insist*, sir," said RSM Rude, bending right over so that his large red nose and little piggy eyes were an inch from Cyril's, "that you take charge – *sir.*"

Cyril got up. "Please don't stand so close to me," he said, backing away. "Look, RSM Rude, I don't think you understand. I am not a soldier. I am a writer. I am not here to fight or train your men. That is your job. Didn't Colonel Clout explain that?"

"No," said RSM Rude. "He just said . . ."

"It doesn't matter what he said," interrupted Cyril impatiently. "That is what he meant to say. He meant to explain that I am here to write a book."

"A *book*?" said RSM Rude in astonishment. "What do you mean – a book?"

Cyril stared at RSM Rude's big, red, blank face with its piggy eyes. He suddenly realised that, as he'd expected, the oaf didn't know what a book was.

"A book," he said again. "A bee-oh-oh-kay. A baahoookoooook!" said Cyril, beginning to feel rather desperate. He made a book shape with his hands and flapped them under RSM Rude's chin. "Ooooook!" he said again. "Ooooook!" And then suddenly seeing the volume of Malaysian flowers beside his bed, he hurried over and held it up.

"This is a book. I am writing something like this. And that's another thing – I can't do that inspecting thing any more. I can't get up at four in the morning every day and also write a book. So now, RSM Rude, if you'll kindly go out very quietly and get on with your parachute jumping, I've work to do."

RSM Rude didn't answer. He couldn't think of anything to say. He only just remembered to salute as he went out of the door.

It was now clear to him that a terrible mistake had been made. A madman had been put in charge of Task Force Ping. A madman who also insulted him, RSM Rude remembered, grinding his teeth with rage. A madman who seemed to think that he, RSM Rude, didn't know what a book was. Baahook indeed.

But what could he do about it? Should he perhaps murder Bonhamy? That was certainly what he felt like doing. But Major Bonhamy was still in the SAS, still an officer. Somehow or other, thought RSM Rude, he'd have to *force* Major pipsqueak, shrimp-squirt Bonhamy to do his duty.

Cyril, meanwhile, had begun to read about the Monastery of Pung. Slowly, over the next few days, he started to learn its extraordinary story. The monks had come from China 2,000 years before. With them they had brought the precious relics, too holy to be mentioned by name. They had also

44

brought the sacred Bo Tree. After every meal, Cyril read, one of their most important ceremonies was to smoke the leaves of the Bo Tree rolled up into long, holy cigarettes.

They had also brought the Giant Pin Bush with them. The spikes were so sharp that the monks used to drop the bush on to their enemies from the tops of towers and often killed them. Cyril looked up the Giant Pin Bush in his flower book. The leaves were silver and the tips of the spikes were purple. Cyril thought it looked rather beautiful.

The monks in the Monastery of Pung never washed. After a few years, Cyril read, they smelt so terrible that when the wind was in the right direction they could be smelled on the mainland fifty miles away. This must have been another reason, apart from the sacred relics, why the Malaysians had been reluctant to attack.

On the morning of the fourth day, there was a knock at his door and RSM Rude came in. But this time he almost tiptoed in.

"Good morning, sir," he said, giving a large, false smile, showing a lot of small, black teeth. "How's the – er – book?"

"All right," said Cyril suspiciously. "What do you want?"

"I wondered, sir," said RSM Rude, flashing his little black teeth again, "if you could possibly inspect the men just once more if I made Muster Parade a bit later?"

"How much later?" asked Cyril.

"Four o'clock in the arternoon," said RSM Rude.

"All right," said Cyril, "I suppose I could once more."

"And do you think you could bring your rifle this time?" said RSM Rude.

"We'll see," said Cyril.

"Right, sir," said RSM Rude softly, saluting as he tiptoed to the door. "See you later."

Cyril was so interested in his reading that he was quite surprised when there came another knock on the door that very afternoon.

Once again it was RSM Rude. "Task Force Ping present and ready for inspection, *sir*," he said.

"Already?" said Cyril. "I thought you said tomorrow afternoon, at four o'clock."

"*This* arternoon, sir," said RSM Rude firmly. "And where's your rifle?"

Cyril looked down at his notes again. "What?" he said.

"Where's your rifle, Major Bonhamy?" said RSM Rude.

"In the cupboard there with my parasols," said Cyril, not looking up. The Monastery of Pung was really turning out to be very odd indeed.

Out on deck under a grey sky and chilly wind Cyril was surprised to see the SAS troops lining the rails each side of the cruiser. RSM Rude led the way over to a large mast which rose from the centre of the deck. Here he stopped and lifted a megaphone that was hanging round his neck.

"Right now, pay attention," he bellowed through it. "Major Bonhamy will now demonstrate a practice parachute jump – as I 'ave explained to you."

"Right, sir," he said, taking a step towards Cyril. "Up the mast."

"What do you mean?" said Cyril, stepping back. "I'm not going up any mast. I've come to look for lice on the men's belts."

"Go – up – that – mast," said RSM Rude, taking another step forwards.

Cyril stepped nervously back and bumped into the mast itself, which he now saw did have a flimsy iron ladder running up it. Beyond it, two burly corporals stood side by side.

"No," said Cyril. He wondered if he could dive through RSM Rude's thick legs and make a run for it.

RSM Rude leant over him. "Do I 'ave to throw you up that mast with my bare 'ands?" he growled.

Cyril looked at the big red hands gripping the megaphone. "Oh all *right*," he said. He supposed he could go up a little way, say ten rungs.

But when after ten rungs he stopped and looked down he saw one of the corporals was climbing up after him.

"A little higher, sir," said the corporal.

Cyril looked up and climbed higher. And then higher. Each time he stopped the corporal said, "Higher, sir."

Cyril shut his eyes. He hated heights and now the chilly wind seemed to be getting stronger. Cyril thought he might be blown off. "Higher, sir," said the corporal.

Finally they reached a sort of crossbar.

"Take hold of that handle, sir," said the corporal.

47

Cyril opened one eye, and then closed it. Level with his head was a small platform and above it a short bar hanging from a wire rope. With great difficulty and with the corporal's help, he managed to scramble on to the platform and get his hands clenched round the bar. Very slowly he opened one eye again.

He immediately shut it. The sight was terrifying. He seemed to be about a mile above the deck. From above his head a long sagging wire rope stretched right down to the very front of the ship. At this far end, a tiny figure in the distance, stood RSM Rude, the wire rope passing just above his head. Other tiny figures, the men of Task Force Ping, lined the rails at either side. In the middle of the deck Cyril had seen something that looked like a small flannel. He felt the mast swaying.

"Hold me tight, corporal," he said. "Don't let go."

"Major Bonhamy will launch hi'self from the platform," came the sound of the megaphone faintly from below, "and 'alfway down let go to fall on to the mat you see in the middle of the deck. No doubt 'e will execute a number of somersaults to break 'is fall. Right, Major Bonhamy, ready when you are, sir."

High above them, far too frightened to listen, much less obey, Cyril clung to the bar, eyes tight shut.

"Jump!" shouted RSM Rude. "Jump!"

Nothing happened. "Jump, jump, *jump*!" shouted RSM Rude, getting redder and angrier. He'd make

48

the little teabag jump if it was the last thing he did. "Jump," he shouted, and then, turning the megaphone to its loudest, he yelled, "PUSH 'IM, CORPORAL!"

To his horror, Cyril felt the corporal's kindly hand let go of his waist. The next moment, still clinging to the bar, he was launched into space.

Down he hurtled. But immediately new instructions were being bellowed through the megaphone. "Let go!" shouted RSM Rude. "Let go!"

But Cyril's hands had locked on to the bar. He couldn't let go. He couldn't even hear anything. RSM Rude might as well have been shouting at an Exocet missile.

Which is more or less what Cyril had become. Faster and faster he shot down the wire. The next instant he would either have smashed into the front of the ship or gone sailing out over the waves.

Fortunately both these nasty accidents were prevented – and by RSM Rude himself. Too slow to move, he received the full force of Cyril's arrival, whooshing from the sky.

It was a fearful blow. Big as he was, RSM Rude was flung a full twenty feet along the deck, knocked senseless. Cyril was shaken but unhurt.

At the sight, a great roar of laughter and applause went up from the rough lads of the SAS lining the deck. They had in fact been a bit shocked at the way RSM Rude had shouted at Major Bonhamy. This was just the sort of thing they'd have expected from the man who'd caught Madam Big – one of the famous "Bonhamy leaps" in action.

As Cyril gave his wave salute and tottered down to his cabin to recover, there was another loud burst of laughter and applause.

Only RSM Rude failed to see the funny side. "I'll get even with you," he muttered, getting groggily to his feet. "I'll 'ave my vengeance, so-called Major Bonhamy."

After the incident of the parachute jump Cyril refused to have anything more to do with Task Force Ping.

"That's your job," he told RSM Rude. "And I don't want you to come clumping into my cabin to tell me what you're doing. I have a book to write."

RSM Rude began to wonder if Cyril wasn't some sort of spy smuggled into the task force by Abbot Ping Po. He started to keep a report on Cyril which he planned to give to Colonel Clout.

As they sailed further south, it got hotter and hotter. Cyril gave up wearing uniform and put on the shorts and gaily-coloured Tahitian shirts Deirdre had bought him.

This didn't bother the tough men of the SAS. Now they'd seen with their own eyes that Major Bonhamy could do the amazing things they'd heard he could do, they didn't mind what he wore.

However, the sight of Cyril's floppy, white sun hat above a deckchair made RSM Rude even more furious. He couldn't forget the way Cyril had knocked him flying in front of all the men. In fact whenever he saw Cyril he wanted to fling him overboard. He could hardly bring himself to salute.

Not that Cyril noticed if he saluted or not. The

more he read, the more interested he became in the Monastery of Pung. It was now clear how clever it was of the evil Abbot Pong Wong or whatever he was called to choose it for his last stand.

The Monastery of Pung wasn't really a monastery at all. It was far more a fortress built to protect the mysterious and sacred relics, too holy to mention by name.

He read how they were kept in a golden casket in a chamber which could only be reached by a short winding staircase. The relics were too sacred for any human being to be with them for long. But the entrance to the staircase was guarded night and day. And there was a stone slab at its foot which could be made to tilt down, throwing anyone on it into a deep hole.

Next Cyril read how several of the courtyards could be made to open down the middle and fling an enemy into large sandpits filled with crocodiles.

Gradually he learnt that the Monastery of Pung was just one huge booby-trap: floors collapsed into underground rivers, boulders could be made to crash from roofs, spikes shot out from walls, and there was hardly a bed upon which the ceiling could not be wound down to crush whoever tried to sleep in it, or a chair which didn't conceal some pointed pin to inject a poison.

"I must say I'm glad there's no chance of my going into this terrible place," thought Cyril, but he decided he would make a list of the main traps for Colonel Clout and the brave men of Task Force Ping. "It's the least I can do," he thought.

It grew hotter and hotter. RSM Rude, purple from heat and rage, bellowed at his men as they jumped from funnels or climbed up nets hung over the side of the ship.

Cyril realised that Deirdre hadn't been so foolish to buy parasols after all. He found a secluded spot at the back of the ship where he could wedge a parasol into a hole in the deck and a cooling breeze blew off the sea. In the distance he could hear the thumps and crumps and bangs as RSM Rude trained his men.

Three days before they arrived at Malaysia, RSM Rude came to Cyril and explained it was time for him to be given more kit. This included regulation SAS equipment for jungle and underwater fighting: sten guns, hand guns, harpoon guns, panga knives, grappling hooks, goggles against chemical fog, underwater torches, et cetera.

But since this was such a large and dangerous operation there was just a chance someone might be captured – particularly officers. They were all to be given equipment to help them escape.

Since Cyril had no intention of doing any attacking he didn't really see how he could be captured.

"I don't think I need any of this special stuff, RSM Rude," he said.

"Them's Colonel Clout's orders," said RSM Rude.

"Oh all right then," said Cyril. He often thought the SAS were just like big children.

He thought this even more when he was given his equipment by Sergeant Bell of Stores.

"Good afternoon, Major Bonhamy," said Sergeant Bell. "Three new items on the menu this afternoon, sir – Knockout Cigarettes, the Stun Pen and a new version of the Blast Ball."

"Oh yes?" said Cyril, trying to look interested.

"You see this packet of cigarettes?" said Sergeant Bell. "Innocent enough you'd think, sir, but in fact the front row is all Knockout Cigarettes. Now in captivity, Major Bonhamy, you'll often be given the opportunity for 'a last cigarette'. That's your chance. Kindly offer your guard a smoke too – taking care to offer from the front row.

"Same with this pen," went on Sergeant Bell. "You'll often be given the opportunity for 'a last message'. Just aim along the nib – so. Lift the filler lever – so. And . . ."

Sergeant Bell had raised the pen to his eye and pointed it at a figure target leaning against a bulkhead nearby. The moment he raised the filler lever there was a faint shoosh and a tiny dart struck the target with a thud.

"Accurate to forty feet," said Sergeant Bell. "Stun a man for half an hour – nasty headache afterwards."

"How clever," said Cyril politely, thinking he had never seen anything so corny.

"Thank you, sir," said Sergeant Bell. "Finally – your bouncing Blast Ball. You pull out this little pin – so. Then bounce your ball into the midst of your enemy – so."

With a vigorous movement Sergeant Bell bounced the rubber ball into the distance. Cyril watched

nervously. What was the sergeant planning to do? Blow a demonstration hole in the side of the ship? Demolish the store room?

Nothing happened. "Naturally, that's a dud, sir," said Sergeant Bell. "But this one could throw a couple of men forty feet. Handy for creating a diversion."

He handed Cyril the small black ball, the pen and the cigarettes. Cyril took them back to his cabin, put them on his desk, and then forgot them completely. So completely, in fact, that they were the cause of an unfortunate accident the very next afternoon.

Cyril had set off as usual for his spot at the back of the ship. Under one arm he carried the Li-lo, under the other his water wings in case he wanted a dip, and the parasol with the tassels.

He was irritated to find the back of the ship was full of men. Nets had been flung over bulkheads, smoke bombs were exploding, the SAS were running up and down with bayonets, yelling and covered with sweat.

"What's going on, Corporal?" shouted Cyril, waving his parasol at all the netting.

" 'A' Company rehearsal for night attack, sir," said the corporal, saluting. "RSM Rude's orders."

"Well you can't do it here," said Cyril. "Go somewhere else. Go to the front deck."

"Can't, sir," said the corporal. "RSM Rude's got 'B' Company on the front deck."

"Cancel it then," said Cyril. "I've work to do here."

"But Major Bonhamy, sir," said the corporal. "RSM Rude gave special orders. Tonight is the finale of his whole training programme. He . . ."

"I don't care what RSM Rude said," said Cyril irritably. "RSM Rude gives far too many orders. And you all do far too much jumping about in this terrible heat. Tell RSM Rude I told you to spend the afternoon by the swimming pool."

When they'd all gone, Cyril stuck his parasol in the deck and blew up the Li-lo. But after ten minutes he realised what he'd said to the corporal was true: the heat was now worse than ever. He decided, after all, to go and work in his air-conditioned cabin.

It was shortly after this that RSM Rude, coming aft to see how "A" Company was getting on, was surprised to find the back of the ship quite empty. He was even more surprised to find the whole of "A" Company lolling round the swimming pool.

"Major Bonhamy's orders, Sergeant-Major," said the corporal. " 'E cancelled the training."

"Did you tell him it was the final dress rehearsal?" demanded RSM Rude, his temper beginning to rise.

"I told 'im just that," said the corporal, "and that was when 'e gave 'is orders – 'Off to the swimming pool' 'e said. 'Off you go'."

"Did he indeed?" said RSM Rude grimly. "I must have a word with Major Bonhamy."

"Mind 'e don't do another parachute jump on yer," the corporal called after him. A hearty laugh came from the boys of the SAS round the pool. This was one of their favourite jokes.

Usually RSM Rude just managed to pretend to

57

laugh too. But this time he suddenly felt very angry indeed. He'd taken more than he could stand from this so-called Major Bonhamy. Bashed along the deck in front of his men by that little shrimp – he'd teach him. RSM Rude, his face as red as a tomato, set off furiously in the direction of Cyril's cabin.

Cyril, meanwhile, was just about to make the most amazing discovery. Hidden in the ancient Greek writing he had found a sentence in old Chinese. Slowly, with his dictionary, he translated it:

IN SACRED CHAMBER
OF MONASTERY PUNG
THE VENERABLE ABBOT
HI WU LAID ONLY SURVIVING
REMAINS – WHICH WERE...

"Good heavens," thought Cyril, trembling, "it's going to say what the holy relics actually are." He read on:

THE MOST SACRED FRAGMENTS,
THE HOLY TOENAILS OF
THE DIVINE BUDDHA....

"Toenails!" cried Cyril out loud in his excitement. *"The toenails of the Buddha* – gracious me." With shaking hand he seized the pen in front of him. But it wouldn't write. "Toenails," he tried to write. "Sacred Toenails."

Clattering along the deck, RSM Rude felt himself swelling with heat and rage. How dare that shrimp Bonhamy cancel the training, mincing about in coloured shirts, twirling a parasol?

"The wimp," thought RSM Rude in a fury, starting to run. "The werp. I'll get 'im. I'll teach 'im. I'll show the little werp."

"Major Werp," he suddenly heard himself shouting, as he hurtled down the corridor.

"GRRRRRRR!" he roared as he charged at the door. "GRRRRRRRRRR!"

It was at this exact moment that Cyril, realising it must be empty, raised the filler lever of the pen before putting it in the ink. There was a "shoosh!" and then a tremendous CRASH as RSM Rude hit the floor. A tiny stun dart was sticking out from the lobe of one huge, thick, red ear.

An hour later Cyril was standing by a bed in the ship's sick-bay.

"If only you'd knocked first instead of barging in like that, none of this would have happened," he said.

RSM Rude, lying on his back with his eyes shut, didn't answer.

"Anyway, I'm very sorry," said Cyril kindly. "How do you feel?"

RSM Rude groaned.

"Sergeant Bell tells me the headache wears off in three hours," said Cyril. "And let's look on the bright side, RSM Rude. At least we know the Stun Pen really works quite well now."

But RSM Rude didn't answer. He simply put his hands over his ears and turned his head to the wall. As he went out, Cyril heard him groan again.

The next morning, while strolling to his position on the rear deck, Cyril met Captain Silkin hurrying forward.

"Morning, Bonhamy," said Captain Silkin. "I'm just going to pick up Colonel Clout and your fellow officers."

Cyril watched the ship's launch speeding across the sparkling waves to the distant shores of Malaysia.

Continuing his stroll, he suddenly decided he'd go and put on his tropical uniform. He wanted to look as smart as possible when he saw Colonel Clout. Although he was quite sure the colonel wouldn't mind what he wore, he didn't want anything to distract from his exciting news – the details of all the traps and springs and devices in the Monastery of Pung. But above all, the thrilling discovery he'd made about the relics – that they were the very toenails of the Buddha himself.

The Attack

Cyril found that his tropical uniform had fallen from its hook and got badly crumpled. He realised that he'd have to get Private Coggins to iron it for him.

The delay gave RSM Rude time to see Colonel Clout first.

RSM Rude, although still shaky from the Stun Pen, had been working feverishly on his report all night.

Colonel Clout flipped through the bulky package in bewilderment.

"I haven't time to read all this," he said, noticing that the last section was headed "Second Attempt on my Life". "Just tell me briefly what's troubling you, RSM Rude."

RSM Rude drew a deep breath. "Well, briefly, sir," he began.

It took him half an hour. He grew more and more excited and angry. Colonel Clout listened in astonishment. Parasols, Tahitian shirts, lolling about on Li-los – clearly all nonsense. RSM Rude was making it all up. He had, thought Colonel Clout, gone quite mad.

However, Captain Silkin had given him a clue. He had described the parachute jump incident to Colonel Clout on their way over in the boat. It had sounded like a typical bit of good, clean, SAS fun but he could see it might have irritated RSM Rude.

When RSM Rude finally finished, the colonel said, "I believe you had a taste of one of the 'Bonhamy leaps' early on, Sergeant-Major?"

"Leap?" said RSM Rude with disgust. "That was no leap. If you ask me, Major Bonhamy is little better than a spy and an 'omicidal maniac."

"Quite so, quite so," said Colonel Clout soothingly. "Still, he does seem to have been pretty effective. But I'll have a word with him. Perhaps you could get him, Sergeant-Major. I believe he wants to see me anyway."

RSM Rude went out feeling he hadn't quite got across to Colonel Clout what a horrible wimp and werp Major Bonhamy was.

But after an excited Cyril had explained the extraordinary discoveries he had made, Colonel Clout began to think both his second-in-command and his Sergeant-Major had gone equally mad.

"Well that's all very well, Bonhamy," he said at last, "I've no doubt these chappies smell pretty bad. Never wash, eh? But I don't see that putting our lads off you know.

"And I don't see how these toenails of yours are going to help us. Not much we can do about toenails except cut them. Ho! Ho! Ho!" laughed Colonel

Clout, enjoying his little joke. "Toenails – cut – oh ho! Ho! Ho! Ho!"

"Very funny," said Cyril coldly. "This just happens to be one of the most extraordinary discoveries about Buddhism ever made. It also explains why Abbot Wang Po . . ."

"Ping," interrupted Colonel Clout.

"What?" said Cyril.

"It's Ping Po, not Wang Po," said Colonel Clout.

"Yes," said Cyril, "Ping Wang Po – of course. It's a difficult name to remember. Anyway, it explains why the abbot has all these ancient traps and pits to protect him."

"Now those *did* sound interesting," said Colonel Clout. "We must know about those. Could you give a quick talk to the men about them this evening?"

"Well, I'm only half-way through my reading," said Cyril doubtfully.

"Do what you can," said Colonel Clout briskly. "There's no time to lose. We attack tonight – or rather tomorrow at dawn."

"Good heavens!" cried Cyril, thankful it would be nothing to do with him. "At dawn? How bold."

"Oh, by the way, Bonhamy," said Colonel Clout as Cyril was leaving. "Have you had any trouble with RSM Rude?"

"Not really," said Cyril. "There was an unfortunate incident with that pen bomb thing they gave me. The stupid man barged in without knocking."

"Good. Excellent," said Colonel Clout. "But don't be too tough on him, Bonhamy. He's more sensitive than he looks."

"Really?" said Cyril. "I must say you surprise me."

He spent the afternoon finding out still more about the Monastery of Pung and adding to his list of traps. He decided that he couldn't give a talk. He'd just give everyone a copy of the list, with a rough map.

It was a lovely hot afternoon and usually Cyril would have done at least some of his work on the rear deck. But he realised that with all the other officers in uniform he'd look a bit odd as the only one not wearing it. He put his Tahitian shirt back in the drawer and the parasol and Li-lo in the cupboard.

Colonel Clout was to address the whole of Task Force Ping in the main dining room at five o'clock. Cyril got 200 copies made of his list and map and arrived at ten to five. The officers were in the front two rows of chairs. Colonel Clout faced them, standing on a little stage. Behind him was a large map of the Island of Pung and a small blackboard.

"Gentlemen, officers and men of the SAS," he began. "As you have already been told, we attack tonight. Please pay attention."

He explained that while Task Force Ping had been sailing south, the SAS officers had done a series of daring raids on the Island of Pung. They had discovered a great deal of valuable information, including the fact that in two days' time Abbot Ping Po was expecting large reinforcements from the mainland. Hence the need for an immediate attack.

"As you see," went on Colonel Clout, pointing at the map with his cane, "the Island of Pung has these 700 feet cliffs at one end and down both sides.

At the other end it is quite flat. Our raids have shown that the cliffs themselves are heavily mined with the dreaded teacup mines. So is the ground between the cliffs and the monastery. But for some reason the flat ground at the other end has no mines.

"Now," said Colonel Clout shrewdly, "no doubt there are traps there. Major Bonhamy has a word to say about traps later. But that is where we shall launch our attack. It will be an underwater attack. Special goggles will be worn for protection against chemical fog."

Cyril found his mind wandering. He could see RSM Rude to his left, in the row behind the officers. Big as the SAS men were, RSM Rude was still bigger. His bristling head, red face and fierce piggy eyes were a foot above everyone else. Cyril thought he looked about as sensitive as a mincing machine.

Now that the time for the actual attack had come, Cyril found he was rather nervous. He'd thought before that he would go in, heavily protected, two or three days after the SAS had captured the monastery. Now he thought two or three weeks would be better.

All at once he heard Colonel Clout mention his name. He was one of a list of officers whose names were being read out. With rapidly growing horror, Cyril realised it was a list of names to do with the attack. Once again the colonel mentioned his name.

"What's that?" said Cyril. "I'm sorry – I didn't quite hear what you said."

Colonel Clout paused and looked down. "I knew that would please you, Major Bonhamy," he said.

"Yes – I want you and RSM Rude to lead the attack on the west flank."

"*What?*" cried Cyril, leaping to his feet as though he'd been given an electric shock. "But I thought you said . . ." He stopped. What he really wanted to say was something like, "I'm sorry, but no. Out of the question. Never." But he could feel that the whole of Task Force Ping was looking at him. Somehow it was too embarrassing to say it just like that, out loud, in front of them all.

"But I thought a plane," he said, as a new idea occurred to him. "What about a helicopter?" He suddenly saw himself safely high above the battle, taking notes. "Hover," he added, waving his hand vaguely in the air.

"Good thinking, Major Bonhamy," said Colonel Clout. "You mean an airborne landing. Parachute jumps – we all know how good you are at *those*."

A gust of rough laughter went round the room. Only a scowling RSM Rude didn't join in.

"I'm afraid Abbot Ping Po's inside defences are far too strong. The only possible method of attack is underwater by sea."

"But," said Cyril again, still standing up. Once more the sight of all those white faces was too much. "But what about the sharks?" he ended in a small voice, sitting down.

"Good question, Major Bonhamy," said Colonel Clout heartily. "I was just coming to that."

"As you know, men," he went on, "the seas round here are full of the deadly White Giant – the fiercest killer shark in the world. Fortunately I have

66

managed to obtain five barrels of Mammoth Whale oil. This doesn't have a very nice smell. In fact," said Colonel Clout, "it smells absolutely disgusting. But no killer shark will come anywhere near you if it smells Mammoth Whale oil."

There were some more orders which Cyril listened to in a daze. Then he explained he couldn't talk about any traps there might be outside the monastery because his parchments were only about those inside. There was a list of these and a map for each man. Finally, when they broke up, Cyril crept miserably back to his cabin.

There could be no question of him taking part in any attack. For one thing, he couldn't really swim. He was only good at floating. You couldn't float into attack. Nor could he use any of those silly weapons they'd given him. He couldn't even lift several of them.

Cyril decided he'd have to hide somewhere until it was all over. To cover his white uniform he put on the black silk dressing gown Deirdre had bought for him and then slipped out of his cabin up on to the deck.

There was a neat pile of tarpaulins beside the spot where he stuck his parasol. Cyril pulled the top one part way off the heap and made a sort of tent into which he crawled.

He lay there for what seemed like hours. He thought he could hear distant sounds of preparation and twice he thought he heard them call his name on the ship's loud-speaker system. Several times he dozed off.

But it was extremely uncomfortable under the tarpaulins. Cyril decided at last that he'd hidden long enough and crawled painfully out on to the deck.

It was empty and silent. No doubt the attack had already gone in. In fact, at that moment the whole of Task Force Ping was drawn up in ranks on the lower deck about to have revolting essence of Mammoth Whale oil sloshed over them.

All would have been well had it not been for RSM Rude. When it was discovered that Cyril was missing, Colonel Clout had at once ordered a search, as well as calling his name over the ship's loudspeaker system.

But there was only an hour before the attack was due to start. And, as Colonel Clout pointed out, Major Bonhamy wasn't the sort of chap to miss a scrap like this if he could help it. Another officer was put in charge of the attack on the west flank.

"I fear something serious must have happened to Major Bonhamy," said Colonel Clout, and called off the search.

RSM Rude didn't believe this for a second. Either Major "the wimp" Bonhamy was a spy, in which case he'd gone to warn the Island of Pung, or else, as RSM Rude suspected, he was a feeble wimpish coward and was hiding. RSM Rude had searched Cyril's cabin several times himself.

Twenty minutes before the attack he decided to have a last look. Thus he was just in time to see a small figure wrapped in a black silk dressing gown tiptoe down the corridor and disappear into the cabin.

Cyril, still in the dark, was half-way to his comfortable bed when to his surprise and alarm the light snapped on. Turning, he saw a hideous sight.

It was RSM Rude. Seeming about nine feet tall, his black wet suit dangling with weapons, a harpoon gun in one hand, goggles covering half his face, he looked like some monster from outer space. He also smelt terrible – no doubt from the foul essence of Mammoth Whale glistening all over him.

"Oh good evening, RSM," said Cyril as airily as he could, holding the corner of his dressing gown to his nose. "As a matter of fact I don't feel too well. I thought I'd give this evening a miss. Just carry on without me. I'll join you tomorrow if I feel better – or the next day."

RSM Rude didn't say anything. He took three steps forward and did what he'd wanted to do ever since Cyril had arrived on board. He seized him by the scruff of the neck, shook him violently in the air and then stuffed him roughly under one arm.

"Ow, you're hurting me," cried Cyril, his voice muffled in RSM Rude's large armpit, squelchy with disgusting essence of Mammoth Whale. "Put me down, you big bully. Let me go," Cyril tried to shout, kicking and struggling.

But RSM Rude took no notice at all. He didn't even pretend Cyril was an officer any more. He simply gripped him tighter and ripped open cupboards and drawers with his large hands, pulling out the Li-lo and Tahitian shirts and flippers, goggles and parasols and weapons and flinging them on to the floor.

69

Cyril realised struggle was useless. He shut his eyes and let RSM Rude shove him savagely into his wet suit and ram on his flippers.

"Where's your Sten gun?" growled RSM Rude, giving Cyril another squeeze.

"I don't know and I don't care," said Cyril. "Put me down."

RSM Rude wrenched open another cupboard and hauled out more guns and knives and belts which he tied and tightened and hooked round Cyril. He seized the Knockout Cigarettes, Stun Pen and Blast Ball off the desk and crammed them into a pouch on the belt. Into another pouch he put hand grenades.

"Where are my water wings?" wailed Cyril. "I'll drown without my water wings."

"Water wings," snarled RSM Rude, wrenching the buckles on Cyril's flippers another notch. "I'll give you water wings, you little wimp. You'll come with me and we'll see how you fight. We'll see how you do your 'Bonhamy leaps' now, you tweep."

Cyril just had time to grab a copy of his list of traps and a map to stuff into a pouch and RSM Rude was pushing him out of his cabin and up the companion-way stairs.

There wasn't time for Cyril to take up the leader's position. RSM Rude simply clipped himself to the last man, and then attached Cyril to him by forty feet of nylon rope. He pulled a pair of anti-chemical fog goggles over Cyril's eyes; over his mouth and nose he fastened a breathing mask and turned on the heavy cylinders. Finally, he emptied a whole bucket of stinking Mammoth Whale essence over Cyril's head. Cyril thought he could smell it even through the mask.

The men of the SAS stood waiting tensely in the darkness. They were in six long lines at six openings in the deck a few feet above the water. Soon each line would pour through its opening, dive into the sea and swim powerfully for the Island of Pung. Cyril's line would be leading.

Cyril himself was wondering if he could sit down. He weighed a ton. He could feel his knees buckling. He could also feel something clammy and ticklish below his neck. Cold, oily, revolting, foul essence of Mammoth Whale was seeping down his body inside his wet suit.

Suddenly he thought he might cut his way free. He was so covered in guns and grappling hooks and rope and stuff he felt like the thing in Deirdre's kitchen where she hung her pots and pans. But at last he found his panga – the deadly jungle slashing knife all SAS men carry on this sort of attack.

Gently he pulled on the handle. Nothing happened. He pulled harder and then harder – with both hands, panting, Cyril yanked and pulled and shook the panga. He could hear himself rattling as all the guns and hooks jangled together.

All at once a huge head loomed down out of the darkness. "Sssssh!" hissed RSM Rude furiously in his ear. "Sssssssssh – shush!"

Cyril let his arms fall to his sides. "I'll soon be dead anyway," he thought miserably. "What does it matter?"

He didn't have long to wait. He heard a sort of

shuffling far ahead along the deck. Then RSM Rude's hand reached back and pulled him forward.

In a few seconds, it seemed to Cyril, they'd reached the opening. One moment RSM Rude was standing blackly in front of him, the next he was gone. Cyril peered down in terror through his goggles, seeing the line joining him to RSM Rude slipping swiftly away.

He could just see the dark waves glinting below. They were miles away. He couldn't possibly jump. He clung to the side of the door. Perhaps the line would break.

He felt it tighten with a sharp tug. Desperately Cyril clung to the ship, his arms wrapped round some sort of knob.

For an instant he hung there, the nylon line taut and quivering, then with a ferocious yank RSM Rude pulled him in.

The other soldiers had entered the water completely silently. Cyril came straight down smash on his stomach. The splash was enormous. Then he sank like a stone.

RSM Rude, feeling the weight of Cyril pulling down heavily behind and below him, realised at once what was happening. At last he saw his chance of revenge. With a vicious slice of his panga, he cut through the nylon rope. Cyril continued to sink like a stone.

And no doubt he would have continued to sink swiftly down through the warm, inky Malaysian sea until he'd reached its bottom, but suddenly there was the most frightful jerk. The next instant he was being rushed through the water at terrifying speed.

"Help," thought Cyril, clinging to his oxygen mask to prevent it from being pulled off; "my line has caught in a submarine or a torpedo. No," he thought, as he seemed to go faster still, "it's an underwater missile. Oh help, someone, help!"

In fact it was a White Giant, one of the huge killer sharks. Racing through the sea to escape the terrifying smell of Mammoth Whale, its tail had caught in a loop of Cyril's nylon rope. A quick flick to free itself had turned the loop to a knot.

Now completely entangled, the shark became crazed with fear. There seemed to be a Mammoth Whale almost on top of it. Fast as it swam the Mammoth Whale swam just as fast. Spurt after spurt the shark put on. Panic-stricken, it thrashed its tail from side to side. Behind it, a roaring in his ears, banged and beaten by the hurtling water, Cyril thrashed from side to side too.

He could hardly breathe, though he clung to his oxygen mask. He felt he was in a nightmare. Pangas, coils of rope, hooks, revolvers, grenades, clips of ammunition, stun bombs, harpoon – everything was ripped from him and vanished into the waters behind.

After eight miles, the shark had had all it could take. It had never known a Mammoth Whale that could swim so fast for so long. With a last despairing flick of its large tail it flung itself through an underwater opening in the rocky cliff beside which it was swimming and flopped down on to the narrow beach of the cave beyond. Then, exhausted, the shark

abandoned itself to its fate. The Mammoth Whale lay beside it, more or less unconscious, too.

But slowly Cyril began to recover. After a quarter of an hour he managed to sit up and take off his oxygen mask and the two heavy cylinders. Relieved of their weight, he was able to stand up and, with great difficulty, undo RSM Rude's many knots and free himself from the line.

It was pitch dark, too dark, luckily, for Cyril to see the still senseless body of the enormous shark. But he took a few feeble steps and realised, from the crunching under his flippers, he was on a beach. The flippers, however, he could not remove. RSM Rude had pulled the buckles too tight.

Feeling himself all over Cyril found that everything except two pouches had been stripped off him in his terrible trip through the water. Miserably, holding his hands in front of him, he started off up the beach.

Cyril very slowly walked – or rather more and more painfully, flopped and flapped in his flippers – for half an hour. He didn't know how far the missile had taken him. Probably about a hundred miles, considering the speed. He was a long way from the Island of Pung, on some remote Malaysian shore. He'd just have to flap along like this till he met some humble peasant, who'd give him shelter and take off his flippers. These grew more and more uncomfortable, especially as he seemed to be climbing some steep rocky path.

Cyril was also aware that he still smelt strongly of foul essence of Mammoth Whale. So strongly, in fact, that he longed for a handkerchief to hold over his nose. Typical of the SAS to load him with ridiculous stun bombs and knives and not think of useful things like a handkerchief.

After half an hour he could go no further. He sat down and pulled furiously at his flippers, but couldn't budge them. He leant wearily against a convenient rock and shut his eyes.

After a while it occurred to him to look into the two pouches still attached to his belt. In one, he could feel the Stun Pen, Blast Ball and Knockout Cigarettes. In the other he found a small waterproof electric torch.

He took this out and turned it on. He found he was in an underground tunnel cut through solid rock.

Cyril got to his feet and started up again. He was slightly refreshed from his short rest and his torch made it much easier. He was also now quite definitely hungry. He'd find one of those primitive but kindly families and ask if he could share their humble breakfast, thought Cyril, his stomach rumbling. Some coconut milk and a colossal ostrich egg omelette or whatever they ate.

Ten minutes later he found himself in front of a small stone door. A single push and it swung smoothly open.

Cyril was at the end of a long stone chamber. There were no windows but it was lit by large candles stuck on spikes. Orange-coloured robes hung on hooks down the length of each wall.

Cyril examined these with interest. They had

hoods and rope belts and seemed very much the sort of thing you'd expect a monk to wear. And on the back of each robe was a large Chinese

This made Cyril extremely nervous. Could "P", he wondered, stand for Pung? Had the missile simply been whizzing round in circles? Instead of taking him, as he'd thought, safely away from the dreadful island, had it flung him right on to it?

He hurried down the line of robes and quickly chose the smallest. This completely covered his head and trailed several feet behind him, but that did mean it hid his flippers.

It was just as well he did so. Moments later he heard high voices, the door at the far end of the chamber opened and about fifty monks streamed in. Cyril shrank into his hood. One look at them and it was clear he had indeed landed on the Island of Pung. For one thing, he could see they never washed. Even their shaven heads were streaked with marks of dirt. For another, they were all armed. These tall, filthy, strong, young men were obviously the dreaded warrior monks of the wicked abbot.

Cyril shrank behind another robe. It was fortunately not one belonging to any of the monks who had come in. Once they were all robed, they formed into a long queue. Cyril was able to join the end as the last monk went through the door. As far as he could tell, no one noticed.

Cyril found the ten-minute journey through the twisting, echoing corridors extremely unpleasant. For one thing, the smell of unwashed monk was very strong, though at least it stopped them smelling Mammoth Whale essence.

For another, it was very difficult keeping up with their long strides in his flippers. By the time they arrived his feet were in agony.

They were in an enormous hall, lit by large candles and filled with long tables laid for some meal. Cyril's stomach rumbled again. He flapped rapidly towards the nearest table. He imagined fighting monks would need plenty of delicious food. Little pheasant sausages, thought Cyril, swallowing, minced titbit of humming bird.

At the far end of the great dining hall he could see a small table on a raised dais at which stood an enormous and sinister figure. This must be Abbot Wong, or whatever he was called.

There was a long pause, while the monks stood in silence, then, at the sound of a loud gong, they all sat down. Each table was now approached by two younger monks carrying between them huge brass bowls from which rose an appetising-looking steam.

But to Cyril the meal was really a disaster. The bowls contained what looked to him like piles of rolled-up socks floating in a lot of hot greasy water. In fact, it was one of the monks' favourite dishes – yam-yam balls in a piping soup of rancid butter and tea. While they guzzled and gulped and had second and third helpings, Cyril gloomily tried to force down another disgusting mouthful. The yam–yam balls even tasted like rolled-up socks.

Nor was there anything else. Just these metal washing-up bowls of muck, the one in front of Cyril still half full. It was ended by another loud bong on the gong.

And there now began what he had been vaguely dreading all through the meal. Each monk bowed low to the monks on either side, and then reaching inside their orange robes they each produced a long, pale cigarette. Meanwhile the younger monks appeared carrying lighted tapers.

It was the smoking of the sacred Bo leaf. Cyril remembered from his reading how important this was; and how important that every monk carry his own holy supply. He was bound to be discovered.

He made frantic movements of searching under his robes. Then he looked at the floor behind him as though his Bo cigarettes must have fallen on the way in.

But suddenly he remembered the cigarettes in his pouch. He reached inside his robes again, pulled it open, took out the cigarettes and shoved one quickly into his mouth. A lighted taper appeared in front of him.

Cyril had two or three quick puffs. There was a short pause, then a series of deafening yells and crashes.

As he toppled backwards, one flipper caught under the rim of the brass bowl and sent it hurtling. Rancid butter and tea poured over the monks opposite him, yam-yam balls flew everywhere.

His second flipper caught the monk next to him a fearful smack in the face and sent him crashing back on to the flagstones.

Beside him, Cyril lay unconscious – orange robes wide open, wet suit, flippers and face all exposed. The Knockout Cigarettes were still clutched in his hand.

The Abbot of Pung

When Cyril came to he was lying on a large wooden bed in a small room with a high ceiling and one small window. He was still dressed as before, in his long robes and wet suit. A huge figure, the one he'd noticed in the dining hall, was watching from the end of the bed.

Cyril knew at once it was the evil Abbot of Pung. About eight feet tall, he was dressed in long orange robes with a pale-green hood. He had a big, thick, hooked nose, and small, wide-open black eyes. While the other monks were shaved bald, the abbot had black hair bound in a top-knot on top of his head.

"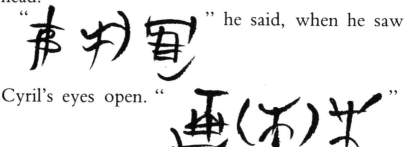" he said, when he saw

Cyril's eyes open. "   "

"I'm sorry," said Cyril, "I parle French bon, and I speak English. That's all."

"So," said the abbot, "Eeeengleesh. You must be one of the stupid fools who tly and attack me. As you saw, I do not even need all my men to defend myself. Your flends have not even got to the monastely. They fall into pits, into wells, clockadiles have them, sharks, snakes."

"Oh dear," said Cyril.

"I do not need you, Eeeengleesh," said the abbot. "Soon I keel you. But I would like to know how many men are coming. Will more men come soon?"

"Well, I don't really know," said Cyril, pulling himself further up the bed away from the abbot.

"I theenk you do, Eeeengleesh," said the abbot silkily. He came slowly round the end of the bed, at the same time drawing an enormous curved sword. "Come Eeeengleesh," he said, "how many men?"

Cyril slipped off the bed and stood nervously in his flippers. "Now look here, Abbot Pang, I mean Pung," he said.

The abbot stopped. "What did you call me?" he said softly. "What did you say my name was?"

"Wung," said Cyril. "Wong . . . Wang. Wing."

The abbot's cruel face twisted with anger.

"So," he said, beginning to tremble, both hands gripping his sword, "so – you choose to insult my name. You insult me to my face. You mock me."

He raised the sword slowly above his head and advanced back round the end of the bed. "What is my name? MY NAME?" He suddenly shouted ferociously. "WHAT IS MY NAME?"

"Pang," cried Cyril desperately, backing away. "Peng – Peep – Pee – Pie – Pish – Posh – Puddle – Pup – Pop – Po – Oh help! Help! Help me, Deirdre!"

With each insulting word the abbot's fury had increased, until at the final "Help me, Deirdre," Cyril had turned and started to run – or rather flop and flap – in a panic round the room.

In three colossal strides the abbot had him trapped in a corner and stood towering over him. He bent his hideous face to Cyril. *"What is my name, Eeeengleesh?"* he snarled.

"Poop," whispered Cyril.

And then, as the abbot stepped back, Cyril remembered the Stun Pen. Feverishly he scrabbled in his pouch, pulled it out, pointed and pulled the filler lever. To his horror, only a thin stream of blue ink spurted from the end and fell between them.

"So now, insulting Eeeengleesh – you die!" cried the abbot, swinging the sword high above his head.

But at that very moment there came a violent hammering and shouting at the door. The abbot paused. For an instant it looked as though he was about to slice Cyril in half. Then he lowered his sword and went to the door. After a few words he turned.

"The last of your companions have got here," he said. "First I finish them. Then you."

When he'd gone, Cyril went and sat wearily on the bed. He threw the pen crossly across the room. Typical of RSM Rude to give him the wrong one. Probably on purpose. Once more he tried to wrench

off the flippers, but each movement – each flapping run, even sending the yam-yam balls flying – had just pulled the buckles tighter.

Cyril gave up and started to look round the room to see if there was any way out.

He was obviously in a very old part of the monastery. The walls were made of huge blocks of stone with curious patterns roughly carved upon them.

It occurred to Cyril that his 1,000-year-old parchments might have told him things about the monastery the monks themselves didn't know, or had forgotten. Studying the now very crumpled map and list of traps, he saw that he was probably in one of the old guest rooms. A number of these had secret exits.

Cyril got off the bed and went to the door. He counted three blocks up and then six blocks along. Putting his hands on one side of this block he gave a gentle push.

There was a faint click and turning round he saw that two of the larger blocks of stone in the far wall had swung inwards, making a low door. Cyril hurriedly flopped across and slipped through it. After a moment the two blocks swung shut behind him.

He was at the top of a narrow circular stairway. A door at the bottom was opened by a simple catch. Cyril wrapped his hood closely round his head and peered nervously out.

It was a long, empty, stone corridor, lit at intervals by large candles. He could hear the sound of gunfire in the far distance.

It was in this direction, orange robes gathered about him, that Cyril now began to shuffle. He thought if he was going to be killed, which now seemed extremely likely, he would rather be killed with Colonel Clout and his men than alone under the sword of Abbot What's-his-name.

He saw only one of the fighting monks. A shaven figure, carrying a rifle and without his robes, came trotting past him from behind. When he heard him coming, Cyril pulled his hood across his face and shuffled even slower so as to keep his flippers hidden. The monk ran past without even a backward glance. Cyril supposed he'd gone to join the rest of them fighting the brave boys of the SAS.

As he went on the walls of the corridor began to be decorated with ancient designs carved into the stone which Cyril was almost sure he recognised from his reading. When at last he came to a T-junction, where the passage branched sharply left and right, he stopped and looked closely at his map. Then he put his head out and looked cautiously in each direction.

It was as he'd thought. To the right, the corridor stretched away until it reached a corner. From here came the sound of gunfire, now much louder.

To his left it opened out into a high, wide, circular chamber, brightly lit with candles. In a row round the walls were twenty carved dragons at head height, their tongues lolling out. At the far side, opposite Cyril, a tall monk stood guard at the entrance to a narrow staircase.

He had arrived at the chamber which lay directly

below the room which contained the sacred Toenails of the Buddha.

Despite the danger he was in Cyril felt he couldn't resist just one peep at those amazing objects. Wrapping his orange robes close he shuffled out into the open and started slowly round the chamber, counting the dragons' heads as he went.

When he'd reached the sixth he suddenly reached out and pulled sharply on a long stone tongue. At once, the slab upon which the monk was standing swung open. He gave a startled cry as he disappeared, a cry instantly cut off as the slab swung shut above his head.

Cyril now hurried forward and started up the stairs. The Toenails themselves, he remembered, were too holy for human presence. He would find no one there.

The room at the top was small and round and had no windows. The walls were covered in thin sheets of beaten gold gleaming in the candlelight. In the middle was a simple marble pillar about three feet high, and on this stood a small casket made of glass and gold.

Cyril went and looked at it closely. It was clear the Buddha had seldom if ever cut his toenails. Certainly he had never washed them. Thick, black, twisted, they were about four inches long. They looked, thought Cyril, more like the toenails of a very old goat. Not a pretty sight.

Still, they would be of great interest to scientists. He would give them to his old friend Professor Nic Hill at the British Museum. Cyril jammed the casket into his pouch and went back down the stairs.

As he hurried along the stone corridor the sound of gunfire grew louder and louder. Cyril was now really longing to re-join Colonel Clout. With any luck, RSM Rude would have been killed. It was clear a big battle was going on. He hadn't been confident enough before. Remembering the great hulking lads of the SAS, it seemed to him now that the monks of Pung would almost certainly be beaten. Cyril hitched his robes above his waist and, as fast as his now excruciatingly painful feet would allow, broke into a sort of jumping run.

It was hurrying that nearly did for him. He had almost reached the corner beyond which, judging from the explosions of grenades and crack of rifles, the battle was going on, when he heard a loud shout behind him. A bullet went smack into the wall above his head. Terrified, Cyril stopped and turned round.

Some twenty yards behind him advanced a party of ten monks. When Cyril stopped, they stopped, chattering among themselves and pointing at his feet. Looking down, Cyril saw his black flippers still sticking out under his orange robes.

The ten monks raised their rifles. Cyril reached frantically into his robes, grabbed the casket and held it above his head.

"Stop!" he shouted. "Sacred Toenails! Stop!"

At the sight of the gleaming casket the monks flung themselves flat upon the ground, hands clasped in prayer. Cyril backed slowly away, holding the casket high. Every now and again he shouted, "Toenails! Toenails!"

At the corner he stopped, drew the casket back behind his head and flung it as hard as he could at the prostrate monks. Then he pulled off his robes and set off in a series of agonising leaps and jumps towards the gunfire.

Nine of the monks scrambled desperately to rescue the sacred Toenails as the casket smashed into pieces among them. The tenth set off after Cyril.

But fear gave Cyril strength. Painful as it was, he bounded down the corridor and out under an archway into blazing sunshine. Then he leapt and sprang on, flippers smacking, right out into the middle of a great marble terrace.

To the monks and men of Task Force Ping locked in battle it looked as though a huge ungainly black toad had hopped clumsily between them. There was a sudden, amazed silence.

Cyril looked round in bewilderment. To his right and below him stretched the ornamental hedges and rare bushes and shrubs of the magnificent formal gardens of the Monastery of Pung. To his left rose three more marble terraces, with broad steps, fine marble balustrades, and every so often, statues. Above these, to one side, stood a colossal eighty-foot golden statue of the Buddha on a tall column.

All at once the familiar voice of Colonel Clout came from behind the balustrade on the third terrace.

"Quick, Bonhamy," he shouted. "Up here. Third terrace. We'll give covering fire." He'd hardly finished speaking when the air again filled with the sound of explosions and the crack of rifles.

Once more, and for the last time, terror gave Cyril

strength. Desperately, his feet feeling as if they were on fire, he flung himself up the steps. As he reached the third terrace, strong hands pulled him to safety behind the balustrade. The noise was deafening.

"Well done, Bonhamy," shouted Colonel Clout, who'd pulled him in. "You've made it."

His face was grimy, his eyes bloodshot. Blood was running down his cheek from a wound by his eye. He looked exhausted.

"What's happening?" shouted Cyril, when he'd got his breath.

"I fear it's the end," shouted Colonel Clout. "Most of our chaps were caught in those damned traps on our way here. Just twenty of us left. As for Ping Po – look for yourself."

Cyril peered fearfully between the little marble pillars of the balustrade. It did indeed look hopeless. Below him, for a hundred yards, stretched the beautiful monastery gardens. Within every bush and shrub, from behind each fountain and statue, crouched the fearsome fighting monks of Pung. There must have been nearly the whole 300 of them. And steadily they were closing in on the remaining men of Task Force Ping.

But Cyril could really only think of one thing now. "Do you have a knife, Colonel Clout?" he shouted above the din. He pointed at his feet. "Scissors would do. It's my flippers . . ."

"Not now, Bonhamy," shouted Colonel Clout, a trifle impatiently. "Get out there on the left flank and see what you can do." He pointed vaguely along the terrace, and turned once again to fire at the advancing monks through the balustrade.

With a groan, Cyril set out to crawl in the direction he had pointed. "If I ever get out of this," he thought miserably, "my feet'll have to be amputated."

But what was happening was so frightening that for a moment he even forgot the torture of his flippers. Bullets whined overhead and smacked into the marble all around him. There was the crump of larger things exploding and showering him with lumps of this and that. Thick smoke was now drifting down the terraces. "I'll be hit soon," thought Cyril. "I wish I wasn't here."

So when he saw through the murk a particularly large SAS soldier sheltering behind the base of one of the statues, he flopped thankfully down beside him. He was less pleased when he discovered it was RSM Rude. RSM Rude was not at all pleased either. He was also very surprised. He'd supposed Cyril to be floating about somewhere or at the bottom of the sea. He paused between throwing stun bombs.

"What are you doing here?" he yelled.

"Nothing," said Cyril. He was lying on his stomach, flippers and arms outstretched.

RSM Rude had a sudden urge to throw him over the balustrade. Instead, with one hand he hurled a couple of hand grenades down into the gardens; with the other he flung Cyril a spare automatic rifle.

"Take this," he shouted.

"Oh shut up," said Cyril, pushing the rifle away. He'd decided to give up. He rolled over and stared up into the smoke. He'd simply lie there until something big landed on him.

But all at once he remembered the bouncing Blast Ball still in his pouch. He'd make a last effort. He'd throw the Blast Ball and then wait for something to land on him.

He got unsteadily to his knees, crawled round the base of the statue and, holding the Blast Ball, looked over the balustrade.

At that moment, with clouds of smoke and showers of splintered marble, something blew up on the terrace directly underneath him. Terrified, Cyril hurriedly pulled the pin and, in his confusion, threw it wildly over the parapet, meanwhile dropping the Blast Ball between himself and RSM Rude.

There was a short pause, and then the most tremendous whooshing explosion.

RSM Rude, much larger and nearer than Cyril, was simply tossed into the air and down on to the terrace below. Luckily his fall was broken by the branches of a Giant Pin Bush growing in a tub.

Cyril, on the other hand, shot forty feet into the air and landed between the feet of the mighty Buddha which towered above the terraces, courtyards and gardens of the monastery.

For some minutes he lay stunned. He was vaguely aware of RSM Rude's bellows of pain, which could be heard even above the din of battle. Then, feeling very groggy, he pulled himself into a sitting position.

The sight below him was a terrifying one. Through the smoke from the explosions drifting down the terraces he caught glimpses of the last brave men of Task Force Ping. Below them, swarming now two-thirds of the way up the monastery gardens, were the warrior monks of Pung. It was only a matter of minutes before they reached and overwhelmed the terraces.

Cyril looked up at the big round golden knees of the Buddha bulging about twenty feet above him. Then he looked ahead of him where ten great golden toes, each three feet long, poked out of golden sandals. The toenail on one of the little toes seemed particularly bright . . . Cyril stared at it, frowning.

There was something very familiar about the statue, and particularly about that toenail. Surely he'd read a description of it in one of the old parchments. He pulled his map and list out of the pouch and spread the crumpled pages. Yes, there it was – "Press down hard on toenail of little toe on left foot."

Cyril's feet were now so painful in the flippers that he had to drag himself forward by his hands. He heaved himself up on to the toes of the left foot and with his remaining strength pressed down on the gleaming gold toenail of the left little toe.

Deep under the monastery garden there could suddenly be heard the rumble of ancient machinery. Then, before the astonished eyes of the SAS, the most extraordinary and spectacular of the monastery's medieval booby-traps went slowly into action.

Grinding and quaking, the entire hundred-yard length of gardens pulled apart, splitting down the middle into two halves. The noise of battle stopped abruptly, to be replaced by cries of terror as the two sides of the garden fell inwards. In sections, each part of the garden now spun rapidly round, hurling the screaming monks into the pit below.

As they landed, silken nets unfurled and fell upon the heaps of struggling men. Cunning counter-springs drew the nets tight. In a few moments all of Abbot Ping Po's men, and the evil abbot himself, were captured – caught fast, netted and secure.

Home Again

There is not a great deal left to tell. Almost the first thing Colonel Clout and his men did was to rescue Cyril from between the feet of the Buddha.

"Well, I can't say it really surprises me," said the colonel. "I knew if anything could save us it would be one of those 'Bonhamy leaps'."

"It was nothing really," said Cyril modestly. "Look, do you think you could cut these flippers off my feet?"

It took them a week to clear up the Island of Pung. The few monks left in the monastery were soon captured. Cyril opened the sliding slab at the entrance to the sacred Toenail staircase and they hauled the monk, bruised but unhurt, out of the pit below it.

They also recovered the sacred Toenails themselves, but Colonel Clout said Cyril couldn't take them to his friend Professor Hill and must hand them over to the Prime Minister of Malaysia.

He had radioed to Malaysia soon after they had

secured the remainder of the monks in the monastery. Crack troops of the Malaysian Army were sent over from the mainland and the wicked abbot and his men were taken away.

The most difficult task was finding and opening all the booby-traps from the sea up to the monastery, about which Cyril had no details.

Eventually, each was found and opened. Not a single SAS soldier had been harmed. They had been unable to avoid the traps themselves, but once in they had been more than a match for whatever they found inside. Adders, scorpions, crocodiles and sharks had been reduced more or less to mincemeat.

The voyage back was very jolly. All the rescued SAS were told about the tremendous "Bonhamy leap" which had saved them. Many congratulated him.

"It was nothing really," said Cyril again and again. He didn't exactly understand how he'd got shot between the toes of the Buddha. He just remembered an enormous and stupendous explosion.

Even RSM Rude, having spikes from the Giant Pin Bush painfully removed in the ship's sick-bay, had to admit a grudging admiration.

"Sorry about that incident in the sea, sir, but I knew you'd prefer to go in alone," he said craftily, when Cyril visited him.

"That's all right," said Cyril who hadn't the faintest idea what he was talking about. "I'm sorry about the Pin Bush. Will it be much longer?"

"Several weeks, sir," said RSM Rude, wincing. "They've still got seventy spikes to go."

HMS *Nelson* arrived home to a terrific welcome. Bands, TV cameras, photographers, huge crowds lined the quay at Southampton. Colonel Clout and Cyril came down the gangway first. Mrs Clout and Deirdre were waiting for them at the bottom.

"Oh darling," cried Deirdre, flinging her arms round Cyril. "I'm so glad you're safe. Are you all right? Next time you go away, I'm coming too."

"I'm never going away again *ever*," said Cyril.

There followed several days of celebrations. The whole of Task Force Ping, including Cyril, met the Prime Minister, who had taken a close interest in the whole venture.

Cyril appeared on five television programmes and gave fifteen interviews to newspapers and magazines. All his past adventures came out, together with photographs.★

But the climax came two weeks after their return. The Malaysian Government had promised a reward of one million pounds for the capture of Abbot Ping Po and his force of warrior monks. This was £5,000 for every man in Task Force Ping. But when they learnt what Cyril had done, an extra sum of £10,000 was given for him to have specially.

It was decided the presentations would be made live on telly in Cyril and Deirdre's house in Wimbledon. Colonel Clout and all the officers of Task

★ To read about Cyril being kidnapped, see *The Terrible Kidnapping of Cyril Bonhamy* (Evans, 1978). To read about his battle with Madam Big, see *Cyril Bonhamy v Madam Big* (Cape, 1981). And for Cyril's terrifying time with the notorious Pierre Melon, see *Cyril Bonhamy and the Great Drain Robbery* (Cape, 1983).

Force Ping would be there. So would Commander Henderson of Scotland Yard, Mr Underline, the Defence Minister, and the Malaysian Ambassador to give the cheques. The Prime Minister had also insisted on coming and making a short speech.

All day more and more people arrived at the house and Deirdre spent her whole time making cups of tea. Vans parked outside and men ran cables to cameras and lights below the new library in the attic and into the library itself.

It had been decided by the producer that it would be nice if Cyril came down the metal library steps, carrying a few scrolls and parchments, to receive his cheque.

A quarter of an hour before the programme, Cyril put on his SAS uniform for the last time. Men ran up and down the stairs to the attic, tripping over cables. Colonel Clout and his officers, Commander Henderson, Mr Underline, and the Prime Minister all arrived in their separate cars.

Cyril was surprised how pleased he was to see all his SAS friends again. "Nice to see you, Colonel Clout," he said.

"Call me Claud," said Colonel Clout, shaking him warmly by the hand.

"This way, please," said the floor manager.

Seven minutes before the programme they were all gathered below the attic in front of the cameras. Lights were blazing. Suddenly the producer had an idea.

"Couldn't Mr Bonhamy *jump* from the attic?" he said excitedly. "Do one of those 'Bonhamy leaps' we've been hearing so much about these last few days?"

Cyril looked up from the script of his short speech of thanks for his cheque, which he was still trying to learn.

"No," he said. He was quite nervous enough without that.

"But just a little 'Bonhamy leap'," pleaded the producer. "Seven million people will be watching this programme."

"I don't care how many people are watching it," said Cyril irritably. "I'm not jumping down those steps."

"Quick," the floor manager said suddenly. "We're on the air in two minutes. Up into the library, Mr Bonhamy. Come down when the red light up there comes on."

Cyril climbed the library steps and pulled them clattering up behind him. There was a short pause and then a small red light came on among the boards of switches beside the floor manager.

Waiting expectantly underneath, everyone heard a loud rattling and shaking from the attic library. The cameras were trained on the trap door. The Malaysian Ambassador stood smiling, holding his cheque.

"Quick, Mr Bonhamy," hissed the floor manager desperately. "*Quick. You're on the air.*"

There was a short pause, some more rattling and then an explosion of deafening crashes and bangs from the attic library as of someone jumping violently up and down on the trap door. Cyril seemed to be trying to smash his way through.

In the silence that followed, the listeners below and the seven million viewers watching could plainly hear Cyril panting and gasping.

"I can't," they heard him call at last, his voice muffled. "It's stuck. I'm locked in. Deirdre, you'll have to call the Fire Brigade."